SHORT STORIES

Sean Patrick Durham

Published by Sean Patrick Durham, 2022.

SHORT STORIES

First edition. December 9, 2022.

Copyright © 2022 Sean Patrick Durham.

ISBN: 979-8223257967

Written by Sean Patrick Durham.

Coffee, Croissants, and Broken Dreams

Sean P. Durham

Introduction

Sean Patrick Durham lives in Berlin. He loves to write fiction, short stories and novel length works.
Stories reflect human life. Our experiences and lives may appear different on the outside, we follow different paths, but everybody's experience of life can be found somewhere written by an author who is thoughtful and observant about the world around him or her.
An author writes observations down in words, so it will, in reflection of reading, mean something to the reader. In other words, we all learn about life by reading fictional lives.

Copyright

Contents

SHORT STORIES

A New Neighbour, a Hot Shower, and a Cup of Tea

A New Neighbour, a Hot Shower, and a Cup of Tea

When I look out of my rear window I see a tree that is as large as the house I live in. I live in a block of apartments with four floors, on each floor there are two doors, each leads to an apartment. Some of these doors represent a mystery to me, I don't know, or am not sure who lives behind them. Mystery always excites intrigue and curiosity.

About half of the doors in the apartment building are known to me; I have at least seen, or met the occupants, talked with them, and either immediately warmed to their way of relating, or quickly turned cold and said "goodbye".

When a new couple moved in two years ago we thought it would be nice to have new neighbours. Inevitably, we would meet at some point on the stairs or at the house door, then greet each other with the normal politeness of strangers.

One day there was a knock at my apartment door. It was my new neighbour. I noticed for the first time that she was pregnant with several months behind her, yet she was chirpy and smiley. She introduced herself and suggested a cup of tea together, just to say hello.

It's a simple and straightforward way to break the ice. I invited her inside, and we went to the kitchen, I noticed a rolled up bath towel under her arm — I didn't ask about it, but after a while I noticed that she kept it neatly tucked under her arm, and as we chatted in the front room and drank the tea, she wouldn't lay the towel down. It stayed under her arm as if it was a part of her normal attire.

Occasionally, as we talked about the neighbourhood, I tried to peek at the rolled towelling. I wanted to see if there might be a pair of swim-goggles or a rubber pool-hat in there. I was sure she must be going swimming later.

She seemed to be an outspoken person, there was an edge to her that I wasn't sure about. She talked only of things external, only about the streets, the shops close to the apartments, and told me that she hadn't met anyone else in the house. I was the first one.

She seemed to have an opinion about everything in the house, how things were done, the rules concerning the backyard where we throw away rubbish. Dividing plastics, metals, and papers into different containers. She didn't like that, we should suggest changes — make it all easier for the people in the house.

She said nothing of her husband or her pregnancy, and I was left wondering about what I should ask and not ask; I asked her how long till the baby is due, and hoped it wasn't too personal.

Three months if all goes well, was the answer. The conversation stopped, we looked around the room, my bookshelves might offer a good conversation, the sound of traffic outside wasn't interesting enough to talk about.

A shout from the street, the hoarse voice of a man rattled against the windows. We looked at each other and laughed for a moment. We speculated about the fuss outside. A man ranting on a street corner, spit filled words, anger, swearing, and another voice replying, "Okay, okay, take it easy. Don't get upset about everything". It then went quiet, a slammed car door, the sound of a motor revved high for a moment, and it was over.

We finished the tea, and I asked if she would like more. She said no. Too much tea, and she will have to visit the bathroom every five minutes. It was bad enough already — due to the pregnancy.

I was about to mention the neighbour opposite my apartment. A man around my age, born in the house and living with his father. The mother died a few days after I moved in. I don't know what was happening, but each morning when I went out, I couldn't help feeling sad as I passed the redundant wheelchair in the hallway.

The son is a dealer. He's okay though, he only deals in the various strains of weed that people use to relax after work. Cannabis, marijuana, grass. All those, and not the other. His clientele is a respectable lot. They come to the door, often professional couples, suits and polished shoes, pressed clothes, not the rag-tag-trade of the street. He does them a good service, and does no harm.

He and I get on well, we always stop and chat a few minutes, talk about what we're up to these days. One night around four in the morning, we bumped into each other on the stairs. He was high as kite. The enormous smile on his face told me everything as he wrapped his arms around me and greeted me like an old friend. He told me how he felt, and that he was glad to know me and that we were neighbours. I think he's a little embarrassed by it these days, but I think it was an honest moment.

I picked up the tea cups and walked to the kitchen, my new neighbour followed. I made body language signs that it was time to say goodbye, I had work to get on with, the cats needed feeding, or I need to go shopping. Just things that people understand as polite gestures of, *I also have a life to get on with.*

I mentioned the towel, now. Feeling more relaxed about pointing towards it, "going swimming?".

"Oh, no. I want to take a shower," She said this easily, without any implications.

"A shower? So, you bring a towel with you for tea, then go home and take the shower?" I asked.

"No, I need to use your shower. Mine's broken — there's no hot water in my apartment. I'm sick of cold showers." She pointed towards the bathroom door, and raised her eyebrows.

"Yes, that's my shower."

It seemed a little odd. I showed a confused expression and nodded to her, against my own consent. A neighbour, a stranger, using my personal facilities before we even get to know each other.

She went into the bathroom, I had to show her how to get the right temperature, and told her to watch out for the slippery surface. I offered her a towel, then she held up the one she had brought with her. I was being overly polite.

While she showered I thought of what might happen if my partner returned home. How would I explain the woman in our shower, the cups of tea, ruffled cushions on the settee? And what if my neighbour across the way saw her leave the apartment after showering, her rosy cheeks and thanking me for my warm welcome?

As soon as she had finished showering, she walked into the apartment, stopped and nodded at me, "That was great!", is all she said.

She was dressed and the towel was now wrapped around her long dark hair. I didn't say anything as she opened the door for herself and went down to the second floor, door on the right. I listened as the keys slid into the lock, the twist and jingle of metal, and the door closed behind her.

The Turkish Baker of Zossener Strasse

The Turkish Baker of Zossener Strasse

There are stories in the streets of Kreuzberg, many of them already erased by the wind. Many lie sleeping in the Bergmannkiez Cemetery.

Some stories persist. They can't go away or be swept up on the wind. These stories come alive each day in the actions of the people of Kreuzberg. They are truths.

Autumn draws fresh cold lines around the neighbourhood of Kreuzberg, it turns the green leaf into a curling dark apple. The sun shines on some days, and dark clouds hang low the next. Nothing is the same in Kreuzberg, this corner of Berlin where people work hard at survival, life, work.

Wet streets and the hiss of rubber on tarmac, shrugged shoulders covered with dark clothes, and the newly paled faces of shivering shoppers. Doors now closed to keep the warmth in and the wet out.

The Bergmannkiez graveyard is full of those who were once local people, they lie in peace. Autumn is no longer on their mind, nothing should disturb their rest, not even the nagging thoughts of change.

I have walked through this graveyard many times, reflecting on the mysteries of life and death.

Life is a mystery that unravels itself, the mundane is only the cover of a book that beckons to be opened and read. Most people, it seems, are too frightened to delve deeper into those ancient pages.

As I walked the paths through the graveyard, I passed a grave I had never noticed before. A simple modern sculpture of two lovers entwined. A man and a woman. She, "Meister Tänzerin", a Master dancer, and he, a Choreographer. For sure a story of love — or maybe not, a story of a jealous muse who broke hearts and kept lovers separated?

Further down the path I saw a cat sitting on the top of a gravestone, peacefully enjoying a single ray of sunshine that warmed the stone for her. I stopped and read the inscription. Sadly, the grave of a young boy, about ten years old when he passed from this life. "Taken by the waters, delivered to the heavens", that was all it said. I presumed it meant that he had drowned. The cat slipped away and disappeared into a small thicket of trees.

As I headed towards the gate at the end of the slope, I passed statues, crosses, graves so long untended that their names had become blobs of moss and lime. Then as I approached the gate I glanced across at the statue that adorned a grassy grave. The dark marble figure of a woman, middle-aged, tired face, and a triste looking hat with a leafy motif embossed on its side, a shopping bag hanging from her fingers. A work of art that depicts a life, a mundane life of cooking, shopping and tending to her loved ones. A life.

I walked away from the wooded graveyard and into the neighbourhood where bakers and hairdressers do their business. A cyclist rushed past, dodged a figure crossing the street, then stopped behind a 40 ton delivery truck, her red face glowed in the cool air, her lips pushed outwards as she whinnied like a horse. She raised her head, and I could see the whites of her eyes as she attempted to get past the truck.

Autumn changes, but stops nothing. It makes us shrug at the shoulders as we make the brisk journey towards the underground stations. Thoughts are of work, play, and keeping going till we can go back to our rightful places of rest. Our eyes see the ground ahead, filled with fallen flattened leaves, cut to shreds by boots and heels.

Eyes dropped to the street, just listening to the grate of metal, the clatter of slammed doors, and the constant groans of mechanical things. The smell of beer when passing the doorway to a bar, a place for drinking all night. No cocktails, just whiskey and beer.

Damp air grabs at odours, it holds them tight until enough people have pushed it away, they walk through the invisible fug with twists and turns of their shoulders, and quicken their step when it's pungent.

The smell of the city, a bit of this and bit of that. The ambiguous clash of everybody's world. Everyday life.

I pass the baker in Zossener Strasse. The Autumn air filled with that familiar smell of bread. The promise of warm food, sweetness in the mouth, the thought of butter slipping, steam rising from the fresh white bread. A moment of joy. The imagination is lit with bright feelings of home.

The baker's lot has changed. More efficiency, faster baking methods, central bakeries with automated-everything to ensure the business is making top dollar, this is today. Tasteless loaves — white blocks of half-baked bread shoved into each other at the end of a conveyor belt.

You don't know if it's cream in the middle, or yellow jam filling — no, it's just not baked. Damn.

When people pass the Turkish baker shop in Zossener Strasse, more than halfway down, close to the corner where you go down into the underground, they know it's good bread. Made by special hands.

If you stand on the opposite side of the road and watch the people on Zossener Strasse, people who are in a hurry, or not, when they reach the baker's shop you'll notice how they lift their heads and sniff at the air, all of them do it. Some of them skid to a halt, look around themselves then step inside, as if an invisible hand pushed them through the door.

Whoever kept going tucked their chin down onto their chests and dug their hands into their pockets. They sniffed at the air for a last pleasurable whiff of bread before they moved on to the underground.

I was watching people on the street. I had my camera, took a few shots, walked about the Bergmann Neighbourhood, then stopped opposite the Turkish baker's shop in Zossener Strasse. There was a line of people, at least four of them outside on the street waiting to get inside. The windows were so steamed up that I could hardly read the signage of large red letters on the window pane. The letters have been carefully placed high to ensure people can look through the glass and see all the breads and cakes in the cabinet next to the glass.

If you stand close enough, on the same side of the street, you get a view of the woman behind the counter serving the customers. Her thick worker's hands pointing at different breads, then holding the bread up for a customer to inspect, fingers and palm like a small cup to receive money, a bunch of coins held between the tips of her fingers and thumb, then, the coins dropped into the customer's palm.

Her face always blocked by the large red lettering on the window. The bread is always in view.

The patient line of feet goes back to the street. The smell of freshly baked bread comes from the rear of the bakery, it shifts in the air, then through to the front, it fills the space where customers silently stand and dream, then it drifts out into the Zossener Strasse, here it is grabbed by the wind and carried along until it mingles with the smells of traffic and people.

I wanted to take a few street shots around the baker's shop. The steamed up glass, maybe I'd be lucky enough to see the vague image of a customer's face through the steam, where the moisture begins to slip and drip down the glass. Every street photographer knows this shot, it's cliche, but it's fun, and it's a challenge to make it your own shot. It didn't look promising, so I moved around a little, leaned on a wall and watched customers come and go. The window was so heavily covered in moisture, and it didn't look like it would start to fade, drip, or anything of the kind, anytime soon.

I waited as customers stepped outside, bread wrapped in warm paper, each one smiled as they gently lifted the small parcel of food closer to their faces, then they walked away into the crowds. Some customers couldn't wait any longer, and so began pulling at the loaves they had bought, they ripped away the thin paper, then tore away chunks of bread.

A group of men stood close to the curb near a red car, one of them leaned against the door and filled his mouth. Another laughed loudly, his mouth stuffed with wet bread. The taste of fresh bread seemed to cheer them up as they ate it. The men stood close to each other but didn't speak, they only ate bread. The Turkish Baker's bread.

It occurred to me that I shouldn't wait too long, and I needed to do something else. The baker was back there, unseen, busy at work. He, or she, whoever, was baking bread for the longest line of customers I'd every seen here. By now, I could see a line of at least fifteen people waiting in the cold, rubbing their hands, pulling at their hats and caps to cover their ears, faces damp and red. The group of men near the car were still laughing, bright faces in the cold weather.

The people in the line at the door waited patiently, silently, one of the men from the group called out, "how long? Anybody know?"

A couple of people in the line turned towards him, one of them spoke, "Like always, when he's done the work first — be patient, man." The customer turned away and stared into the doorway, he was next to gain entry. He had to wait until the woman at the counter waved him in.

As I watched him, I could see his feet shuffle, he put his hands into his pockets, then removed them, he rubbed them together, then let both hands hang loosely by his sides. A woman came outside, she joined the men, she held the bread up above her head and waved it around for a moment. The men laughed together, she stepped up to the red car and tore the wrapping from her bread, then a chunk of the crust. The men breathed in deeply, smiling at the woman as she placed the first warm bread in her mouth.

The bakery is clearly special. But once, it wasn't much of a shop, just another baker selling sweets and breads. Now, it has something rare about it — fresh bread baked by a master baker. A quality that everybody loves.

Zossener Strasse is one of Berlin's older streets, and like so many Berlin neighbourhoods, the structures and buildings, bombed and flattened in the war, were then used as foundations for a new era.

Apartments and shops went up quickly, the Government promised that in ten or twenty years they would rebuild them more solidly.

German orderliness and craftsmanship prevailed, and the quickly built houses proved solid and lasting structures that still serve their purpose today.

The Baker's father moved into the neighbourhood in the 1950s. He was an immigrant worker, offered the chance to make a living in Berlin, he took an opportunity and moved into a small flat above the shop. He kept his ears and eyes open, and then one day managed to negotiate a price for the shop below his home. He worked there as a simple Baker — the trade he had learned, he taught his son the same trade, but with the money they made he could afford to send his son to a school where he learned new techniques of baking, using modern science.

The son learned well, but never forgot the human touch in his work. He put his heart into everything he did, even the day he saved a child from a lake. Or that's what people say about him, he saved a child from drowning, or he didn't, nobody is sure. The Baker is too busy working to tell people his story.

I walked away from the baker's shop. My thoughts were wrapped up in ideas of street photos, cool shots, and catching a moment of life on the street. Something spontaneous might happen, I hoped that I'd find another steamed up window and see a dripped face to photograph. I went to the café on the corner, "Que Pasa", a place where hipsters and dudes go to drink cocktails, eat Spanish food and sit outside. I looked for a composition to frame. A curved back, creased jacket, with angled legs under the table talking to another "shape".

I stood back, about twenty metres, adjusted to 35 mm on my lens, and panned the rows of tables, then the window — which wasn't steamy, then took a shot of a couple leaning into each other at a table. The woman's elbow had caught a white plate, its contents slid onto the chequered table cloth, she hadn't noticed — she was looking into her lover's eyes. Nice shot, look at it later. I heard a shout and turned around.

At the traffic lights behind me, a cyclist was waving her hand at a car driver. The lights were red and the car driver had pulled in too tight to the curb, waiting to turn right into Bergmannstrasse.

The cyclist was angry because she couldn't get past, she wanted to overshoot the red light into Bergmannstrasse. She was screaming at the driver, "Arschloch! geh mir aus dem Weg!" — "Asshole — get out of my way!"

I raised my camera to get a shot of her emotional face, hands flapping about, obscene gestures. Hold the frame, adjust, and wait a second until the perfect composition of bike, obscenity and anger form a memorable street shot. A little piece of Bergmannkiez character on my hard drive. The cyclist kicked the bumper on the car.

I took the shot. Nice moment.

The driver opened his window, poked his head out and looked at his bumper, then back at the cyclist who was now spitting words a dozen at a time. His hand came out holding a leather wallet which flopped open, an identification card. The cyclist stopped swearing, stopped gesturing, and pulled back in place behind the car. Nice and gentle, no fuss, obedient, and no more obscenities.

I heard the driver speak in calm tones, a few words, "Polizei,"- "on a charge if I have to get out of this car..." and then the window closed, the car pulled away into Bergmannstrasse.

I slipped the camera into the bag on my shoulder, and shoved my hands into my pockets. A woman standing on the otherside of the road, a boy by her side, they looked at the spot where the incident had taken place. Her tired face, slightly rosy and wet couldn't hide the heavy rings under her eyes, her dark raincoat open, the belt unbuckled, and each end flopped around like snakes when she turned and spoke to the boy. He looked up at her and listened. They both looked across at me, she smiled and the boy waved. I didn't know them.

They turned, and walked towards the underground, they plodded along the Zossener Strasse, weaving in and out of foot traffic. The boy gripped the woman's hand firmly, so I was sure it must have been his mother. Their steps were heavy and sometimes the boy inverted one of his shoes and scuffed the top leather against the tarmac.

As they drew level with the Turkish Baker's shop, the boy noticed a man standing close to the shop door. The man's dog was tugging hard on its leash, and the man stretched the leash while trying to get the dog under control. The group of men and the woman, still eating their bread, leaned against the red car, and laughed at him. The boy pointed, and pulled at the woman's sleeve. She turned her head towards the man and the dog, then simply pointed to a courtyard gateway next to the baker's shop, her arm flopped down to her side and she tugged at the boy's hand so that they could move on. The boy searched about, his head swinging back and forth, he laughed out loud when he saw the cat. I heard his gurgling laugh from twenty metres away, other people heard it too, they looked over at the woman and the boy.

We all saw the cat, its white teeth grinning, red lips tightly formed. Its back was high and shoulders low, it looked frightening when it stepped out from the gateway to display its fluffed up tail, the dog edged back, then forwards, it barked constantly, the tight leash holding it back gave it courage, but not enough to risk the cat's claws.

The commotion caught the attention of a few other people and they started to walk across the road towards the Turkish Baker's shop. I watched a man who had been busy staring at his newspaper for a while look up, when he saw the crowd forming he threw the paper into a nearby bin, and stepped out into the road without looking. Zossener Strasse is a busy road, I thought he was going to get hit by a bus, and he would have to go to the underground. But he seemed to know what he was doing and made it to the other side without a scratch.

I walked across the street towards the Turkish Baker's. The boy's gurgling laughter seemed to rise above the traffic, the voices, the humourous gasps of other pedestrians. They gawped, exchanged comments, and pointed at the man and the dog who was losing control of his angry pet. The boy's laugh sounded like water tumbling down a drainpipe. Glug-glug-gurgle-gurgle, followed by wet splashes of chaos when it hit the metal grate at the bottom. The woman had stopped and waited patiently by his side.

The boy coughed, spat onto the road, then wheezed loudly. People close by watched him gasp for air. An old man in a flat cap placed a hand on his own chest and breathed in deeply. His grimacing face and blue lips full of empathy. The boy finally stopped coughing.The crowd carried on eating their fresh bread and chatted and laughed. The boy was fine.

The woman leaned over and rubbed the boy's hands, which were a deep purple colour with streaks of whiteness at the knuckles. His face was now wet, so was his grey school shirt. He wore dark trouser which were heavily creased. As I got closer to the shop front, I could see the crest of a school badge sewn onto the boy's shirt pocket.

I lifted my camera to take a shot, but as soon as I looked through the lens, I only saw the woman looking directly at me, wagging her finger. She was admonishing me for my audacious street photographer ways. Bad timing, not now. I lowered the camera, and nodded at her and the boy. I felt like a stranger at a funeral.

The woman was slightly overweight which caused her arms to bow around the sides of her upper body, the open raincoat revealed a purple blouse that looked grubby where the buttons went through their holes. I saw that she wore stockings, one of them had slipped down to her ankle and formed a dark bundle of meshy material that was stopped by what looked like muddy house shoes.

I couldn't make out her hair , although I'd guess it was dark, she wore a felt hat that somehow matched her rosy cheeks and dark ringed eyes, it was a hat for a sad day, but a sprig of green leaves gave it life. I'd seen those leaves on my walks through the graveyard.

The boy tugged at her hand and they walked to the shop door, the woman looked inside, then back at the boy. She went inside the shop, and from what I could see she strutted through to the back, where the

Turkish Baker did his work. The boy stepped aside and waited in front of the shop window. His face dropped to look at the tarmac, he seemed to be searching around with his eyes, as if he didn't know where he was, or maybe he felt alone without the woman by his side.

I moved into the now large crowd that gathered around the door of the Baker's shop. There was a straight line of silent customers waiting, but many people had already bought their bread, not all the same sort; long breads, short crusty rolls, flat Italian bread with a dab of flour across the crust, and the German half rounded loaf of white — too many types to count or remember.

The customers were now chatting as well as ripping at pieces of bread, mouths filled with bread and words, always with laughter the punctuated their muffled sentences. The man with the dog was staring at the red marks across his palm where the leash had raked his skin, the dog sat obediently and looked up at him.

It was so loud that nobody heard the shush-clunk of my camera shutter as I took a few shots. I decided to look at the photos later, the people were beginning to shove each other, in a friendly way, but a bit too much for my liking. I put my camera back in its bag, and stood among them.

Then the noisy voices stopped, without warning or reason. A voice boomed from inside the shop, "The boy, here?" — "Yes, he couldn't wait much longer," a woman's voice said.

"You should have taken him straight to the underground, it would have been better for him." The Baker's voice.

The crowd moved back from the shop door and made space,they agreed with the Baker's words. The long line of waiting customers shifted aside like a wave forming into a rippling wake.

A small man stepped out into the street. His large strong hands pressed against his white overalls. A long dark moustache over his upper lip formed into small upward curls at each end. He pushed his chin in deeply, so that it formed a double roll of skin under his jaw. He could have been a sailor by the way he walked, but it was obvious he was the Turkish Baker. He looked around but didn't seem to notice the men and women who chewed their bread. But he saw the boy crouching at the corner, stroking the graveyard cat, the Turkish Baker walked over to him and held out his floury hands.

The boy stood up, looked at the baker's hands and touched them. The boy's face glowed with delight, his eyes brightened and he looked up.

"This can only happen once, and it'll do no good. You know that boy?" Said the Baker.

The Baker and the boy looked across at the woman who had brought him to the shop, she nodded once then touched the leaves on her hat.

"I wanted to feel you lift me again, it made me feel safe when it happened," Said the boy.

The Baker placed his strong hands around the boys ribs, gripped tightly, and lifted the boy into the air.

The group of men near the car pushed through the crowd and watched as the boy was raised up above their heads. Mouths opened and bread fell to the floor, nothing was said.

The Turkish Baker put the boy down and folded his arms. His moustache covered his lips, but his eyes were soft enough to show friendship to the boy.

"I lifted you out of the water, and it didn't help you, and it can't help you now. You can see that, can't you?" Said the Baker.

The boy bit at his lip, and churned his arms against his chest. The woman took his hand.

The Turkish Baker stood at the door of his shop, then waved the crowd away to make space, he watched the boy walk along side the woman.

They made their way along Zossener Strasse, up towards the graveyard, maybe she wanted to pick some fresh leaves for her hat, or the boy needed to take the cat back to its rightful place. They were walking back to their rightful place in the underground.

Coffee, Croissants, and Broken Dreams

Coffee, Croissants, and Broken Dreams

She descended the stairs quickly, she had all day. It was a rainy Saturday morning, she wanted to relax. Sit in a cafe, alone, drink coffee, maybe a croissant. Then wait for the phone call.

She walked along the street. She had no time for slow coaches who blocked her path. Her heels clicked, she stopped and pushed the cafe door open, looked around and chose a table next to the window. She could watch the street while she waited for the call.

The call would come through, it was important. Her career depended on it. She had a good agent. She had made the right choice.

Her friends had had agents. She would get hers now.

She ordered a croissant and some coffee.

"Can you warm the milk?"

"Yes"

"Not too much, just above room temperature."

"Okay."

"Anything else?"

"No. Wait. Yes."

"What?"

"The butter should be cool — from the fridge."

She opened her bag, took out her mobile phone and checked the battery level. Fully charged. Good, happy. The call, it would come soon. What time did he say, she can't remember the agreement about time. Surely they had said a time.

She frowned. Her fingers nervously rubbed the surface of the table.

She felt the cool air brush her face, the door opened and a man walked in. She liked his dark jacket, expensive. She looked out into the street. Maybe the silver Mercedes, maybe that was his.

She looked down at her dormant phone, and anger threatened to rise in her. She had waited long enough. She suppressed her feelings.

Maybe that was the agent, not a phone call, a visit. That could be it.

She tried to catch his eye, but she couldn't see if he noticed. He was smiling, happy to see her. She calmed herself, he doesn't know her. She was nervous and making assumptions. Stop. She looked at the phone. Frowned and pushed it to the edge of the table. She noticed the empty seat opposite her.

He could sit there. She mustn't be pushy, agents like to power play, do things to worry their clients. He'd want to keep her on the hook, but use her talent. Let him play his game.

She allowed him to sit at the table he'd chosen. She watched as the waitress brought him coffee and two croissants. He cut into the bread, then split the rest with his fingers. As he buttered the croissant, she noticed the flakes of brown crust stuck to his fingers and wondered what he would do about it.

She looked down at her table, searched for the serviettes. Why don't they lay out serviettes anymore?

She raised her arm above her head and called out, "waitress! Can you bring me some serviettes?"

The waitress, carrying a shiny metal tray, stopped and looked at her, then nodded. She brought the serviettes.

"Here's the paper towels you wanted, okay, sweetheart?"

"Serviettes. I asked for serviettes." She pushed her fingers into the pile of white tissues, "but these will have to do, thank you."

The waitress was walking away, but she called out after her, "Please don't call me sweetheart — I'm an actress, didn't you know this?"

She lifted a serviette from the pile, then held it between her fingers. She saw a small stain on the paper, she ripped at it, then it was gone. But now there was a hole that bothered her.

When she looked across at the man, she could see that he was an agent. Surely he'd seen her. She'll hand him a serviette. Then he'll know, they'll recognises each other.

She stood up, told herself to stay calm and walk, hand him the serviette and return to her table. He'd get it, see her, and come to her table after she seated herself again.

She reached his table then stopped. He looked up at her and smiled politely, his face questioned her.

She waved the serviette in front of him, then laid it onto the table. He looked down, confused.

"You don't have any, I brought you one," Then she pointed at his buttery fingers.

He picked up the serviette, then wiped his fingers, and said thank you. His soft voice surprised her.

She returned to her table. She didn't like his soft voice.

Agents should have strong, confident voices that everybody can hear. That was something she was sure about.

She saw him move his head, he wanted to look. She knew this. They always look in the end. Power plays. She knew how an agent worked.

He looked, she looked back at him and smiled, then she couldn't help herself. She waved once. He looked away and shook his head while he looked at his mobile phone.

He seemed to be scrolling through his numbers. Maybe he was looking for her number. He'd surely have it.

She should have been straight up with him, confident. Told him immediately who she was. She would have said, 'I'm the actor, the one you want. I have talent you can use.' Then she would have offered her hand, they would have shook hands, he'd have offered her a seat. Then he would have told her how surprised he was, definitely talented, you're just what the agency needs.

It had happened before, long ago. She had been told by agents that she had talent. They put her on the books, used her talent. She was doing well back then.

If he's planning to call her from his table, maybe to assure himself that he's in the right place, the right cafe, then it would be alright, she would accept his offer, she supposed.

Her face became tight, and her eyes swelled a little. She'd been silly, lacking confidence. Why hadn't she spoken outright, introduced herself to him straight away? She always ruins her chances, right at the last moment. Always when it counts, she buckles, draws away and waits too long. She consoled herself, she was shy, always had been. You have to be tough in this business, never give up.

She watched as he put his phone away. He drank the rest of his coffee, and for a short moment he looked at the serviette. She thought he was smiling, but then she saw him scowl. His face pinched, then reddened. He stood up, then he walked to the counter where the waitress leaned on a pile of cake trays, he paid and gave her a good tip.

She watched him go out. She expected him to climb into his silver Mercedes, but he walked along the street. She watched him, as always, until he melded into the shadows.

Dark Thoughts of Curiosity

Dark Thoughts of Curiosity

When you go to bed at night and turn off the lights, do you notice the change in your thinking?

Your eyes strain to see into the darkness around you, you wish for the moment to come when your eyes adjust. You want them to stop bulging in their sockets so that you can relax and sleep.

The shadow of the half open door seems so large, the slopes of dim moon light are so weak, and the play of shadow and light jiggles your mind into a world of fantasy.

It's impossibly still, yet you are sure that something is moving at the edge of a shadow. You close your eyes. Silence. The tension is too much, so you have to open them again and peer into the darkened room — just to be sure. It may have been a movement, not your imagination. It's the time for burglars. There are stories of strange things happening to people who live alone, you don't want those things happening to you.

People claim to experience visitations at night. But not you, it couldn't happen to you — such a down to earth person.

The mobile phone next to the bed lights up. Its bright screen illuminates the lamp shade and casts a red shadow onto the wall.

You slide your hand out from under the bed covers and fumble as you grab the phone. There's no message. Nothing. Why did it light up?

Why is the mind attracted to shadows? You try and focus on the shaft of moonlight cast between the gap of those flimsy curtains. Maybe you should get up and open them wider, just to help you settle for the night. Better not.

The shadows of life are the mysteries that intrigue the mind. From them, we create thoughts of what might be, what could be. Ideas and strange occurrences sit in the shadows. We have to be vigilant, keep watching the darkness to be sure it doesn't envelop our souls.

Your thoughts flip to day time, you think about the people you spoke with, the food you ate, and the things you read. You try and force the day time into your mind, to fill your thoughts with mundane activities. An hour passes. The shadows are darker. The moon has dipped behind the rooftops and your room is black.

Eyes start to pop and roll. You don't know how long it's been, but it seems like hours since you climbed into bed. The phone next to you has lit up again, you refuse to look at it. It could be *nothing* again, and that makes you think bad things.

The silent hour has arrived. No car passes, no bus. The creaking sound of a lone cyclist echoed along the street one hour ago, it was a cold sound that reminded you of winter. The room is filled with a chill now, and the shadows are shifting — shadows don't move. But the one you are looking at changes its form. As you stare at it, deep into its blackness you see swirls and flickers, like darkness in the darkness. How can that be? Is there anything darker than dark?

It must be close to dawn, that will change everything. The sky outside, you can see through the gap in the curtain. Black sky, no stars, no clouds to see. Your bulging eyes are tired, so very tired now. Your back is twisted into the wrong position, your neck aches from craning into the room's dark pools of nothing.

The shadow by the door shifts again, a small glint of light sparks in the night and begins to play. The room's atmosphere fizzes, a clicking comes from the corner where the chair is. That was somebody sitting down, leaning back into the leather desk chair. Your muscles tense.

You see nothing but what your mind tells you to see. Your bulging eyes see what they know is there, a figure in your desk chair. They are still, staying quiet. Is this a visitation? They stare at you through the darkness, you can feel their eyes, not bulging, but penetrating everything. They stare, the way a ghoul, or a visitor stares without shame or guilt. It owns you. You know this, your mind tells you this. The mobile phone lights up, this time there is a beep. It must be a message so you pick it up.

You keep looking into the dark corner of your room. If the chair moves again? You don't know.

You open the message and a photograph appears on the screen. Probably a meme, or news item from a sleepless friend.

You push yourself up and peer at the screen. There is a photo of a darkened room, you see the lamp that appears like moonlight on your own desk, your chair is occupied by a dark figure in the photo, and all you can see is their gloating eyes lit by the light from a phone screen in their dark hand.

The figure in the photo begins to fade back into darkness. Pixels fizz and their form changes, they seep into the shadows and the screen becomes dark again. The chair in the corner creaks coldly, like winter. Someone stands up, and now, they are walking in the darkness of your room.

Jelly Beans & School Playground Love

Jelly Beans & School Playground Love

Two kids are talking, it's cold enough to freeze the balls off a brass monkey, and the teacher who's doing monitor duty refuses to allow the kids into the classrooms. When the sports whistle signals that break time is over, the kids can go into the warmth. Apparently, freezing your knees off in winter is good for you.

The boy is pulling at his braces that hold up his shorts. His dad told him, men wear them, and it makes you look dapper. He hates them because the clips that adjusts the length are cutting into his shoulder muscles and making his arms feel fuzzy. The girl is staring at him while he twangs the elastic braces outwards. She thinks he's stupid.

The girl grabs at her pigtail and puts it between her teeth. She chews on it, and asks the boy what he just said.

"The sun is shining — even though you can't see it", The boy looks up at the sky, it reminds him of his dads string vest, grey streaky bits with white knotty patches.

"That's a load of rubbish," the girl looks up and her pigtail falls from her mouth, "it's all grey. The sun isn't shining, so you don't know anything."

The boy squints at the sky. He's trying to find a patch of yellow among the grey and white streaks. He points at a yellow patch.

"Look, see that?"

The girl spins on her leather soles and looks up, "That's just a yellow cloud, stupid."

"If you squint your eyes at it, it starts to get bigger and all the grey bits go away", said the boy.

"Oh yeah, bloody hell. You're right", the girl puts her hand across her forehead, she half closes her eyes and peers at the yellow patch. Her eyes begin to moisten and the patch of sunshine cloud turns into a dripping watercolour.

The boy watches her, he's glad she stopped calling him stupid, now she accepts that he knows about things.

"So where's the sun?" asked the girl. She places her pigtail back between her teeth and gnaws on it like it's a corn on the cob.

"It's hiding, behind the clouds — but it's really there. The sun can't go away", the boy twanged his elastic braces, tried to adjust the metal clip. The clip is solidly closed and his tiny fingers aren't strong enough to open it. He gasps at the stinging pain in his shoulders, and his knees tremble because of the cold air.

The girl asks, "so how come it's so cold?" She's rubbing her arms and legs which are now red. Her lips tremble as she chews her pigtail.

The boy avoids answering and looks across the playground.

The girl follows his gaze. The teacher is strolling up and down the white line at the edge of the tarmac square. She's very tall and wears a long pencil skirt, a thick cardigan, she has a whistle tightly gripped between her teeth, she looks at her wrist watch all the time, then rubs her hands together.

"You can also tell what time it is when you look at the sun", said the boy, he now regretted saying this, he would have to prove it to this smarty-pants girl.

"Prove it — what time is it?" The girl grinned at the boy. His eyes rolled upwards, and he rocked his head from side to side.

He looked across at the teacher. She had stopped walking, She stared at the watch, like a cat watches a mouse. The frown on her face tipped him off.

The whistle was now firmly clamped between her teeth, she puffed her cheeks out. In a moment they would hear the scream of her sports whistle, and when it stopped, the kids would gallop away into the warm classrooms.

The boy looked up at the sky again. He could only make out the stringy vest that reminded him of his dad, and the aching in his arms, the patch of yellow cloud had disappeared. He rolled on his Tufty Club shoes, thinking of the animal footprints he'd be able to make when it snowed.

He pretended to scan the sky, and managed a quick glance at the teacher. Her cheeks were now rosy red and puffed out, he noticed the watery look in her bulging eyes — if she didn't blow the whistle now, she'd collapse any minute — the boy squinted, rubbed his chin like a professor, then looked earnestly at his girlfriend, "The sun tells me it's exactly ten o'clock, a.m. in the morning." He twanged his braces and grinned.

The girl looked at him, doubt in her shivering lips.

The teacher stamped her cold feet, her chest rose, and she finally exhaled the pent-up air into the thin shaft of the ceramic sports whistle.

The noise of screaming children abruptly stopped, kids playing tag immediately ground to halt, they stood like statues as long as the whistle pierced the freezing morning, a group of singing girls broke off in the middle of "ring-a-ring-a-roses, a- pocket-full-of-posies".

A girl stood still as she chewed on her pigtail, her lips quivered in the cold, and she wanted to smile and laugh at the boy twanging his braces. She liked him, she had a smart boyfriend.

He knew things about the sun, so that was smart enough for her.

She also knew that he had a bag full of Jelly beans in his pocket, so she was a smart girl, too.

The Portrait Photographer

The Portrait Photographer
"Ethel? Well, that's a nice name — old as wood," Said Rebecca.

"My parents wanted a daughter with a woody sounding name, I suppose." said Ethel.

Rebecca placed a tripod at one end of the room, then attached her camera to the top plate. She looked through the viewfinder at an empty chair. The chair had a soft seat with a flowery pattern woven into it. She stopped twisting the lens when the flowers looked sharp and colourful. Then she stepped back, turned to her client and asked her to sit in the chair.

"Oh, already?" Asked Ethel. She stood up, flapped the chiffon shawl around her neck and marched five paces towards the chair, she twisted her body as she attempted a graceful turn in front of the seat. Instead of delicate grace, a dull thud rattled some glass objects on a shelf as her backside hit the chair.

"I thought you would first talk to me. You know, get to know your portraitee before deciding on poses, and so on," Ethel rearranged her shawl. Rebecca noticed the small holes in the material, and decided it was probably as old as Ethel herself.

Rebecca looked up from her camera lens, "We can talk a little, but I get my best ideas in action. When you sit in the chair, we'll be halfway there — just act naturally, can you stop doing that with the shawl, please?".

"Well, they should be very good photos. I've got an audition for a part soon, the director will probably look through my portfolio before I read for him. And I've heard things about him, you know."

"Really, what have you heard?" Rebecca was still busy adjusting the flash units and soft light boxes. She spoke absent-mindedly.

Ethel flapped a piece of shawl around in front of herself, "He demands a high standard, and has little patience. Only the best tread his boards," Ethel waved the long white shawl like a ship's sail, part of it was spread across her knees, and the rest bunched in her right hand.

"I image he'll want to see emotion in these photos.", Said Rebecca.

Rebecca leaned down behind the camera, adjusted the focus, checked the angle of the two flash units, and placed her index finger gently on the button.

"Are you good? At acting, I mean," Rebecca waited, eye and hand steady, breath baited for the moment.

Ethel's backside rose up from the seat, there was a light puffing sound as air escaped from under her, her face reddened and her eyes widened. Ethel's mouth quivered for a short moment and Rebecca pushed the button, then Ethel, face infuriated and deep red, gave Rebecca an opportunity to push the button and capture three more emotions. One of surprise, followed by astonishment, which then transformed into embarrassed anger.

Ethel stood in front of the chair, the shawl wrapped tightly around her arm, "Of course I'm good at acting — that's why I audition regularly. What on earth do you think of me?" She raised her voice and the glass objects in the cabinet tinkled.

Rebecca snapped off two more shots of Ethel standing indignant. The wide angle on the lens grabbed at her red face and pulled it towards Rebecca's camera.

"I think you've ruined my portraits, haven't you?" Said Ethel.

"I'm sure I haven't. They'll be just what you need."

"Please, turn the chair at a ninety-degree angle. Towards the window light.", Rebecca held her arm straight in front of herself, and wiggled her finger back and forth like a metronome.

The light spread across Ethel's face. The strong snobbish features, and the large rise on the bridge of Ethel's nose were perfect. She looked like a boxer in a mink coat and lipstick.

Two shots.

"Stand up, please. I need you very close to the camera," Rebecca looked in her camera bag. She found exactly the lens she was looking for.

"What on earth is that thing?" Ethel looked shocked.

Rebecca had found the lens on her travels in South America. A woman who lived in a small cave sold it to her. The woman explained that it was a special lens, for a special photographer, "you will capture souls with this lens," The woman had taken a small sum of money, then scurried back into the darkness. Rebecca became curious, so she used it a few times, then discovered its exact use.

On her way back to Europe she had to show it to a customs official who thought it looked strange, "What does this part do? Why does the glass look like the eye of a fly — it has dozens of angles on one surface?" Rebecca couldn't explain, but she was finally allowed to board her flight back home.

She first used it to take some photographs of a woman she didn't like. The results pleased her. After the photo shoot, the woman became very placid, almost soulless. Then she turned angry for a few minutes. Luckily, the woman then simply disappeared.

Rebecca fitted the lens.

"That's it, it won't take long now".

"Oh, I suppose you want me to smile or something, I'd like to adjust my lipstick, first," Said Ethel.

"Can you do rage?"

"Rage? You want me to show anger and torment?", asked Ethel.

"Yes, please. It'll help me to bottle all of your emotions into one simple shot, then I can pack you away for the day," Rebecca looked at her hands and noticed how they sweated with nervous excitement.

"Come on, I'm sure people find you extremely irritating most of the time," Rebecca pushed the camera forwards. The lens was now in front of Ethel's face.

"Is that necessary?" Ethel was angry, a puff of air released from the chair cushion as she attempted to stand, Rebecca pushed her back into the chair. The glass objects tinkled in the cabinet.

Rebecca pushed the button, the camera mechanism slid open, then a metallic clunk that sounded like a guillotine hitting the block.

Ethel had left the room, body and soul. Rebecca busied herself by collapsing the camera tripod, then carefully cleaning the strange lens. She detached it from the camera and placed it into the canvass bag which the woman in the cave had given her.

After cleaning up, she took the memory card from the camera and transferred Ethel's soul onto another memory stick made of glass. The contents could be seen. Ethel's anger and torment hadn't quite reached a point of rage, but Rebecca could clearly see the surprise and shock on Ethel's face.

She went to the cabinet, placed the glass memory stick next to the others and closed the transparent doors again. She would upload it to the computer for a better look, later.

The phone buzzed, Rebecca had made several appointments for the day. She would be busy.

Dark Stories from Between the Cracks of Time —

Dark Stories from Between the Cracks of Time

The man took the key and pushed it into his pocket. Yola came back to the bar, and smiled at me. She had a glint in her eye that I'd never seen before.

I heard a very low humming sound coming from inside somebody's pocket. One of the two men sitting at the table behind me pulled out his phone and clicked a button.

The phone stopped ringing.

The man standing at the toilet door put his phone away and walked towards the bar. He stopped next to me. I looked at him, he was tall, and looked like he spent a lot of time doing bench presses. He looked down at me, nodded, then asked Yola to get him a drink. She put the drink on the counter, he walked along the bar and prodded at a customer who was snoozing, the drinker's head supported in both his hands, eyes closed. He rocked in his cupped hands, then looked up at the robber, surprised.

"We're closing, so get on your way," Said the robber.

He watched the man stand up, stagger, and then make his way to the door. He hadn't paid, but Yola let him walk.

The robber did the same with each customer. Some of them were too drunk and didn't understand that to follow his instructions was better for their health than to sit and argue over the dregs in their glasses. He grabbed them by the shoulders, dragged them across the bar then pushed them out into the street. He was direct about it, but kept enough respect to ensure they didn't try and fight back. They got the message, and moved on to another bar.

The two other robbers sat at the table behind me, they sipped at their tea, and waited till everything was right. One of them looked at his mobile phone again. It was buzzing lightly. He clicked a button and listened for a moment, then he quietly said, "Okay, Weasel. we're here," He slipped his phone into his pocket. He stared at Yola, then the robber who was throwing people out the door.

The bar was almost empty, I sat on my stool. I'd already made my mind up that I wasn't leaving. Two reasons, the first was that Yola would be left alone with these robbers. I didn't want that to happen. Secondly, I hadn't finished my beer and I wanted at least five more to get blitzed enough to send me to sleep that morning. Driving a cab in the night time city can put your brain on full-alert, it's hard to wind down. I don't know any cabbies who can just quit driving after all those fares, each one of them a bag of problems, or aggressive, and always looking for something, and then crash into bed and sleep like a baby. The drink can douse the flames of thought and help you forget the night.

I ordered another beer as the big man threw the last customer out onto the street. Yola hesitated, then thought better of asking me if I was sure. She tipped the brew into a tall glass and put it onto the counter in front of me.

The robber came and stood next to me, leaned over, and in a friendly way, said, "You should just leave. We're closing up, now."

I just told him straight that I'm staying, and explained that I'm doing what I do, drinking after a hard shift of dealing with scallywags and basket-cases. He smiled, then asked me where I came from. He had heard my accent as I spoke German. I told him.

He then asked me what I was doing living in Berlin. I told him. I used to be in the British army. The old story, I met a woman, fell in love, married, then fell out of love. And now, I'm a cabby who lives alone with his television and books. I could see that he was interested.

The two robbers finished their tea, stood up, one gripped a heavy looking tool bag made of canvas. I watched them pass me, they walked behind the bar and lifted the cellar door flap. As they descended into the darkness, I saw a logo on the side of the bag, the print of a hedgehog, and the words, "Boss Hedgehog's Motor Shop".

As soon as they were down in the cellar, the robber standing next to me pushed a button on his mobile phone. He spoke as soon he put it to his ear, "Okay, get on with it, it's okay up here."

Immediately after that, the sound of hammering could be heard from the cellar. It surprised me, but they didn't seem concerned about the clunking sounds they made with their hammer and heavy chisel. Then it stopped. A few moments later they started drilling. The slow grinding noise vibrated along the floor boards.

I don't know how to crack a safe, but this wasn't how it was done in the films. I looked at the robber, he was sipping on an orange juice with ice. He put his glass down, smiled at me, and asked me about cab driving. It was a normal bar-room conversation with another drinker. He suggested I should probably go home, but I refused. Then, his eyes lit up.

He looked at the street through the large glass windows. A Polizei patrol vehicle slowly moved along the street. It stopped. The driver wound down his window and peered into the bar. The robber hit a button on his phone, his face turned red and sweaty.

He spoke to the safe crackers down below, "stop, do nothing. Cops are outside," The drilling stopped, they waited.

I said, "Don't worry about it, they always do that."

"Do they? How do you know?" He asked.

"This is that type of bar, the people in here are pimps, robbers, and local nut-jobs. The cops are looking for likely-faces," The robber nodded his head. It made sense, the place was a dive. Of course, the cops were looking for an easy collar.

"Really, I mean it. It'll be okay."

I realized I had just helped a criminal do his job. I hoped that I was right about the police patrol. The cops weren't moving, and the driver looked like he was preparing to get out of the vehicle. He picked up a clip board and looked at it. Yola looked over at me, the robber was fumbling with his mobile phone. He clicked the button and spoke to the safe crackers.

"Rabbit? Start packing up, it doesn't look good."

Before he clicked the hang-up button, he said, "Tell Fox to look for a back door," They had nicknames.

Rabbit and Fox, and the sweaty robber standing next to me, probably called Hedgehog. Amazing what comes out of the forest at night.

I watched the cops, but tried to look as if I was in conversation with Hedgehog and Yola, I nodded at Yola a couple of times, for no reason, the Hedgehog raised his juice glass and toasted to something or another. I was still aiding and abetting. Couldn't these guys do the job alone, without civilian help?

The cop in the driver's seat spoke with his colleague, then threw the clip board onto the dash and fired up the wagon. They drove off slowly, without looking back.

The Hedgehog told the Fox and the Rabbit, downstairs, to carry on. The sound of a deep sigh rose up the cellar steps, followed by German cuss words. The slow drilling started again, the Hedgehog kept looking at his phone, occasionally, he would call them, and it sounded like they told him to go to hell, let them just get on with the job. They were having trouble with the drill. The job was turning out to be tougher than they'd thought.

The Hedgehog turned to me, he wanted to speak, but he didn't. He looked at the table closest to the door.

"Yola? Why is that guy sitting there?", He looked at Yola.

Yola looked across at the table. An old man in a long coat sat drinking a glass of beer.

"I didn't see him come in, I don't know", She said.

"Well, you served him a beer, He needs to go", Said Hedgehog.

I thought it's none of my business, the job and everything, me helping too much. So I kept quiet. I hadn't seen the man come in, and I hadn't seen Yola serve him a drink.

I did notice that Hedgehog was making mistakes. I shrugged my shoulder at all three of them, and drank some beer.

The drill sounded laboured. I expected to hear the sound of a broken drill bit, at any moment.

The old man turned to all three of us, he nodded at me as if he knew me. His beady eyes were alert, shifting back and forth as he checked the bar. The Hedgehog walked halfway across the bar room, but stopped close to the edge of the counter. He appeared to sense something, a reason to stay away from the man.

"Listen, the bar is closing. So, take your beer and go somewhere else, will you?" Said the Hedgehog.

"Don't worry son, you're screwing everything up, anyway. I'm not the spanner in the works for you" Said the old man. He pulled at his coat, and looked down at old beer stains on the floor.

"You're doing a grand job of fluffing this caper yourself. Let me drink my beer." The old man turned away, gripped his tall glass and surveyed the street outside.

"I don't know what you're talking about", The Hedgehog looked scared.

Hedgehog went to Yola, she leaned over the bar, and he whispered something that I couldn't hear. Hedgehog put his hand on Yola's shoulder. I watched. It wasn't the touch of a stranger, a robber that frightened her. It was a well known touch, just as the way he spoke her name, as if he'd called her Yola a thousand times before.

I realized I didn't need to be here, protecting Yola from dangerous robbers. Nor to help, when the police arrived later. That was all going to be a ruse. A set-up between the inside and the outside, the keys easily obtained from Yola, no questions and, I supposed, a wad of cash for Yola when they made their getaway.

The Hedgehog had a new plan. The old man had put his spikes up, put the jitters into him, he was trying to fathom who this man was, but couldn't. Nobody knew him, or how he'd come to be in the bar. Worse was, he knew about the robbery. That was a bad thing. The old man, poor sod, had knowledge and seen faces that he could talk about.

The Hedgehog told Yola to open the cash register, and give him all the money. She looked shocked.

"No, that'll put me deep in the crap with the owner, the police. They'll all know something's up," now she'd let the cat out of the bag. I heard her say it, more or less admitting to a conspiracy with the animals of the forest.

Yola looked across the bar and caught my eyes. Her forehead crinkled into a frown, then a nervous smile. Her lips shifted and pursed into the form of the *shush* word. I understood it. I had to be quiet about everything.

It was the old man that bothered me, his safety. What the hell was he doing here. I watched him for a moment, he gripped his glass firmly, and slurped the foam off his beer. His tongue popped out now and again and licked his lips.

Hedgehog was fishing around in his pockets, Yola leaned on the cash register, she watched Hedgehog struggle with his mobile phone as he shoved it into one of his pockets, to free his hand. Then he dug deeper into his inside pocket, finally, he found what he was looking for. He pulled out a small gun. It had a barrel that rattled when he moved his hand, it was old and scatched up all over.

Yola uprighted herself, and took a step back towards the rows of bottles, behind her. Her face pale now, and her hands trembled.

The old man sniggered into his beer, then hissed.

I couldn't do much. I had a feeling I should hide, or take cover, but that wouldn't do much for me in this small room. I looked at my glass of beer, and for some reason that I can't explain, I suddenly had a tremendous thirst for it. I picked up my beer. Hedgehog moved his hand, and the barrel rattled. I saw the gun pointed at me.

The sound of the drill in the cellar stopped. A loud crack from a hammer blow filled the bar, then one more hammer blow. We heard the sound of heavy steel hit the floor. The Fox and the Rabbit laughed, and hedgehog's phone started buzzing. He answered, his gun hand went a little limp, he listened, then smiled once.

Hedgehog looked at Yola, "A couple of minutes, then we're out of here," He said, "Give me the money from the cash register," He knew it would be a problem for Yola. She wouldn't be able to explain the stamp on the time line. But he didn't care, he was now getting all the money. He'd deal with Fox and Rabbit when they brought the bag upstairs.

As it turned out, I heard later, she was supposed to open the register thirty minutes after the robbers had left. She would keep the money as her pay-off. That would leave a timing imprint on the computer that showed the owner, and the police, that the robbery had happened later than she reported. If everything was done perfectly, it would give the robbers enough time to get clear of Berlin before the cops started looking for them.

Now, she knew she would still have to make the call late, if not, she would have to deal with the Weasel. And Yola didn't want the Weasel getting upset with her, she'd heard about his methods.

When the police eventually figured that something was out of whack with her story, they'd arrest her, and she'd be back in prison for a long stretch. Yola didn't want to go back to that darkness.

Hedgehog turned to Yola, and pointed the gun at her, "open it, the register!".

Yola clipped one of the buttons and the register popped open. Hedgehog grabbed at the notes and stuffed them into his pockets. He even scraped up the big coins with his large hands. Yola watched every move. He stepped closer to look into the slots for more money. Yola grabbed at his arm, then the gun.

I heard the barrel rattle, then a shot. Bottles shattered, and whiskey dripped to the floor. The gun fell from Hedghog's hand, he backed away from Yola. She was leaning on the counter. Her breathing heavy, confused by the shot, she checked for blood. She hadn't been hit, but there was blood and whiskey on the floor.

Yola bent down and grabbed at the gun. Hedgehog backed off, and slipped into a chair at the same table where The Fox, The Rabbit, and he had at first sat that morning. He was bleeding badly. His shirt wet with blood. He couldn't feel pain, but a rising fear that he'd made a terrible mistake gripped his mind.

The old man stood in the middle of the room. He looked at The Hedgehog, his black eyes dry, lips wet from the beer.

The Fox and The Rabbit came up from the cellar. They carried a shoulder bag with the night's takings. It was a good haul, and had been worth the trouble. The drill bit had broken at the last moment, but the hammer had finished the job, and the door prised open.

They walked into the room and stood next to the old man, he greeted them both with nods and a faint smile.

The old man spoke to them, "Take it out to the van, the white one with dark windows. Then wait a minute for me, I won't be long."

Hedgehog looked up at the old man, he was confused and frightened.

"What's this? It ain't your job to have, old man." Hedgehog dropped his chin onto his chest, the blood was oozing down his shirt.

"I told you, son, you made too many mistakes. You're too cocky, moving about on my patch".

The old man put his empty glass on the bar, and signalled to Yola to get out. She put her jacket over her arm and walked out of the bar to meet The Fox and The Rabbit.

The Weasel stood close to The Hedgehog and looked down at him. He sniffed the air, then made a snapping sound with his teeth. The

Hedgehog curled back into the chair, his chin tucked down low, both hands pushed against his wounded chest.

"This whole job was mine from start to finish, I decided that when The Fox came to see me about it. He was sly enough to check he wasn't hunting in my territory."

The Hedgehog's eyes flickered as he looked up at The Weasel.

"I thought you didn't like rabbits, either?" Said The Hedgehog.

"I don't. He'll find out about that, soon enough."

END

The Thing that Happened to My Snooping Neighbour

The Thing that Happened to My Snooping Neighbour

Rustling paper, tearing, ripping, followed by the flop of a heavy envelope landing on my desk made me realise that I wasn't really alone in my little room.

I had just woken up. It was deepest winter and my whole body, including my head, was hidden under the Swedish quilt that was big enough to cover a horse.

I pulled back the quilt, just enough to see into the room. I saw a dark figure, a man, he stood with his back to me. He was shuffling a stack of my letters as he stood by the window. He scrutinising the letters for clues.

As my eyes adjusted to the daylight, I saw that he was my neighbour who lived one floor above.

I wasn't afraid. He was looking at my mail, and he used his fingers to open each letter, then snoop at the contents. I didn't think he had weapon, he wasn't that type.

When ever I'd talk to friends of mine, I'd refer to him as, "My Idiot Neighbour Klaus".

I watched him, some letters interested him more than others. He stooped as he read the addresses, a shift of his neck and he was looking at the date in the top right corner. Next thing, the sound of the adhesive tearing away from the paper, a little gasp of breath, and the flip of paper as he spread the letter out in front of him.

I could see he was reading a hand written letter. I knew which one. That upset me.

I watched him for at least two minutes before I got up from my bed. I stood up in underwear and tee shirt. I noticed that he'd separated the letters into two piles on the desk in front of the window.

He was concentrating hard on reading the address on an envelope in his hand, he held it up close to his face, adjusting the distance for his focus. He shook its contents, then he groaned loudly. He seemed to lose interest, he threw it onto one of the two piles.

I knew he was a gossipy man. Anything else I knew about him was that he was a retired dancer, slim framed, he used camp gestures like fishing bait, it depended on who he was talking to as to how much bait he put on the hook. He always wore eye liner. I think he believed it made him more attractive to young men. It didn't, it would often become wet and drip below his eyelids and make him appear foolish.

I knew when he shopped, when he ate, and when he left the building, day or night. He was my neighbour, I would know these things.

He would often catch me on the stairs when I left the building. For sure, he wanted to share some juicy titbit with me. He seemed to have a lot of knowledge about many people in the neighbourhood. I can't stand a gossip.

He'd told me everything about the previous tenant who lived in my apartment. They had a relationship, it turned sour. He explained that he had to take action. Nobody else was interested, so he made sure the tenant couldn't come back again. Then he began to miss him.

He'd taken this new tenant, a student, into his confidence. Then lured him with theatrical looks and a limp wrist, which developed into tea on Saturday mornings at his apartment. And just in case the new resident lost his apartment key, my neighbour convinced the student to hand over a spare for safe holding.

After a while, the student realised that his new friend, my neighbour Klaus, had abused his trust, and had been going into his apartment while he was away. He asked for the key to be returned.

My neighbour deemed this to be a betrayal of his trust. He became angry.

There was a big argument between the two of them. It seems that my neighbour had fallen in love with the student, and couldn't bear the thought of being pushed away.

The argument spilled out into the hallway, doors were opened, people shouted, and they were told to shut up and go back inside.

Two neighbours from the third floor, claimed they witnessed Klaus storm into his apartment, then return with a heavy skillet in his hand. He took a swipe at the young student, who stepped back in time for the skillet to miss him and smash into the door.

The young man then sheepishly went back into Klaus' apartment. The door closed, that was the last time that anybody saw the student.

I'd heard about all this because I'd visited the property manager hoping to get an apartment in this nice building. But My Idiot Neighbour Klaus, kept on about it to me. He didn't know me.

A few days later, my neighbour told the other residents that the young student had packed and left. Apparently, in a huff. He left behind a skateboard, an iron, and a strange looking television-set, they were all still in the apartment when I moved in. I have no idea what to do with these things, it was only later when the dust had settled, that it occurred to me that he wouldn't be coming back for them, at all. My mind gets confused.

Often, when I was on my way out, I'd hear Klaus' door open quickly, and while I locked my apartment, his door would slam, and he'd scamper down the stairs and "accidentally" bump into me.

He introduced himself on the first night I moved in. He'd always act with great surprise. He flapped his hands around like a signalman as he spoke, then he would stop talking, and look intently at me, his eyes glistened as if he'd been drinking. The eye liner made everything worse for him.

He was an expert at dragging me into conversation, but he was irritating. But when he greeted me, he was polite. If I stopped and showed interest, he'd gasp, flap open his fingers and lightly place them onto my chest, then start gossiping. I didn't have the time for it, but that's how I got Klaus' version of events.

I think a lot of the stories, the gossip, are embellished versions of simple facts. But I'm not sure of those facts, I think they've been distorted to protect someone.

As he continued to check my mail, I slipped on a pair of jeans. I was surprised that he didn't hear me. His body language told me that he thought that I wasn't home. Maybe he believed the puffed-up quilt on the bed was empty.

He breathed heavily, wheezy, and he mixed it up with various gasps and sighs. He reacted to my letters as if he was reading a best selling novel.

I felt more upset than afraid, he couldn't punch a piece of paper, let alone a person. There were no iron skillets in my room. So I was okay.

He walked over to the student's strange looking television set, and touched it gently. The skateboard leaned against the side of it. He looked down at it, and placed his forefinger on the base plate. I'm sure I heard his breathing increase, like an animal panting. It raised my hackles and made me feel annoyed.

I had a feeling that visiting people's apartments when they were out, was something he did often. He seemed too relaxed and sure in his actions. There were times, when I'd returned home from a night out, and immediately feel as if someone had been in my apartment. In those times, I walked around, looking for signs of mischief, but found nothing.

It fascinated me to observe a person doing something wicked. Invading a neighbour's private space. I knew no real harm would be done, but I would later have to chastise him for his actions by explaining things to him, and then getting rid of him.

I stood and watched for a minute longer. Then I walked towards him, two paces. He raised his head and looked out into the garden. Scuffing my feet on the carpet was loud enough, but he obviously presumed it was a person walking past the outside window.

I coughed. He turned around, his glassy eyes, framed in eye liner, glared at me. Then I saw that he was wearing pink lipstick, a little smear at each corner. He had white powder on his face and rouge on his cheek bones.

"Have I caught you in the act?" Was the first thing that came to mind.

"This is my apartment, my home, why are you here?" I asked.

He wheezed loudly, gasped, and said, "You left your door open. I brought your post."

"The postman does a good job of it himself."

I looked at the letters on the table and saw that there was a personal letter, the handwriting was from a friend who was in prison. He had been found guilty of murder, circumstantial evidence, but it worked for the jury. He would be locked in his dark cell for a long time, and I enjoyed reading what he wrote.

"Somebody could have stolen the letters," he said, then he looked at the floor. That's when I noticed he was wearing a silk dressing gown, like people did in the twenties. The silky belt hung down to his knees, he touched it with his fingers.

"I wanted to know if there was a letter from my student friend, that's the truth," When he said this, his eyes rolled from side to side.

He was caught light fingered. The rouge on his cheeks seemed to grow redder. Not a drop of sweat to ruin his powdered face. He was enjoying himself. I hoped that it would soon turn to fear, then he would leave.

He twisted the silk belt around his forefinger for a moment, then spooled it up around his hand.

"Why do you have my friend's TV set, his skateboard?" He asked.

"Why shouldn't I? You got rid of him so efficiently. It seems that he didn't want them anymore." I said.

" I'd like to know where he is. Do you know? Have you had letters from him?"

He pulled at the silky belt, twisted it, then let it hang like a swinging bridge between his hands.

"I talked to the police that night — the night he disappeared," He said.

"What was their opinion?" I asked.

"They're suspicious. Not of me, but of another person in the block," He said.

This was news. I thought the visit from the police was a simple gesture of officialdom.

"Have they been back, since?" I felt a shiver.

"I talked to the detective on the phone. He'll be back when he knows more," He looked at the skateboard and frowned, "I know what's going on around here, even the detective told me what he suspects."

"This detective, what's his name?" I said.

" You can't speak to him. His enquiries are ongoing."

"I just don't like people who snoop. I get upset."

"Upset?" He stepped back and accidentally kicked the skateboard.

I grinned.

"Detectives, nosey neighbours, all the same types. I get upset," I hoped he would leave. I didn't want things to take a turn, not here in my home.

"I know a lot. I think I know about you," He walked across the room, and stood in the doorway that led to the kitchen.

"I'm a blank sheet to you, and let's keep it that way," I said.

"That letter, the one from the friend in prison. He's no friend of yours. He has evidence that you framed him. I read it all."

"You shouldn't speak that way, you don't even know the man — he's a murderous lunatic."

He stepped back into the room, he looked overly confident as he pointed at the table and the letters, "He writes regularly to you, I read all of them, each time I came here, there was a new letter from him," He smiled, his powdery face cracked. "He's begging you to help him and you don't help. What type of person are you?"

He went to the desk and picked up the letter. He began to unfold it, and as he turned towards me, I picked up the skateboard, and weighed it in my hands, it was suitable.

He began to speak, but I have no idea what he was about to say, the skateboard smashed into his mouth so hard his words turned into gasps followed by that same horrible panting sound he'd made earlier.

It didn't take long. I'd done it before, and I was getting good at it. The student seemed nice at first, but I did need the apartment more than him.

Klaus wasn't a nice man, he treated that poor student like a pet, then abused his trust. So, I kept bashing him in the mouth with the skateboard. It snapped in half just as he died. A lucky break.

In the end you just need a good excuse to deal with bad people, then get on with it. I read that in a book.

So, fair's fair.

The Gangster Who Sat in My Chair

The Gangster Who Sat in My Chair

The thing about a gangster is that you never know what they're thinking. That's how they want it to be. They control everything around them, they intimidate everybody around them. Then, they know, and you don't.

A few days ago, I walked into my local cafe. I hadn't been there for a while, and I wanted to sit, think, and dream a little while I drank coffee after coffee. I do this.

I spend hours in the seat, my eyes drift through the windows and I watch the people pass. My table is close to the window. If the sun is shining, I see it reflect in the passing faces, if it's raining, I can see the drops on the window, and people outside become shifting wet shadows.

I have three mobile phones. I use them to run my business. I sit at my table by the window, watch, and do business.

People ask me what I do, but I don't think that's their business — it's my business. I keep things that way.

One time, I was sitting there watching the street and I saw someone I knew from long ago. An ex girlfriend. She ran along the street holding a soggy newspaper above her head. Her clothes were soaked through, her face screwed up, and I could see how wet her shoes were. I don't know why she was running that day, but way back, when she and I were together, she always seemed to be running.

I walked into my cafe, nodded at the waiter, then went to my window table. A man sat in my chair. I didn't expect him to be sitting there.

I knew he was a local gangster. He controlled a lot of things, and he got people's hackles up until they gave him what he wanted. He liked using violence. He was an impatient man.

It's the cafe's chair, but I like to think it's my chair, my hideout from the outside world. He shouldn't have sat there. I do my best business right there in that chair.

I asked the waiter, "How long has that guy been sitting at my table, how long will he be there — do you know?"

The waiter smiled. He nodded at another table, his smile was like friendly advice. You know, when somebody doesn't want to use words, they make a face, do as if nothing's up, but you better see the signs they're giving you.

I walked to another table. On the way over, the man in *my chair* watched me walk across the cafe, he didn't smile. He looked at me as if he was telling me to 'deal with it'.

I understood, anybody can sit anywhere. So I sat in another chair. I didn't want to lose sight of my table. As I walked, I saw he had a mobile phone on the table in front of him. His blood shot eyes flickered each time he looked down at it.

I got coffee. I watched him. Sometimes, I saw past him and looked at the street. The line of vision was all wrong, so I ended up staring at my coffee, then at him. He noticed. He turned his head, and took a peek at me.

He had short black hair, with strange looking patterns shaved into it. Barbers do the weirdest cuts these days. His hands were plates of meat which he kept close to his lap. He leaned back in the chair, and looked at his mobile phone. I watched him. I wanted my chair.

He seemed vigilant, but self assured. Not tense, not at all tense. That surprised me.

A woman walked into the cafe. It was starting to rain. She shook her umbrella, glanced at me, then she turned to the umbrella vase which stood next to the window table, she saw the man sitting at my table. He looked at her with a blank face. Then she turned, then went to the rear of the cafe and sat down. Her wet umbrella lying on the floor next to her table.

The waiter went to her, he said something, she nodded. It looked like a serious conversation. The waiter got her coffee and a cheese roll.

It was odd. She looked shocked when she'd seen the gangster. It seemed to spook her.

He turned and looked in my direction again. His face had a scar across the chin, and another above his eye. The one on his chin was worse, it was jagged. I imagined somebody had hit him with a broken bottle. Maybe long ago.

When he looked at me this time, his eyes strained a little. I noticed the puffiness in the muscles around his eyes, like someone who hadn't been sleeping well.

I finished my coffee, but wasn't ready to leave. I was waiting for an important phone call.

The waiter came over. He moved my empty cup, then started to wipe the table down. I raised my hands while he turned the damp cloth across the round wooden table. It was an old table with scratch marks from years of coffee cups.

The waiter looked at me, then at the man. The man looked out of the window.

"Just relax and drink your coffee, you can't keep staring at him. You piss him off, and he'll make your life hell."

I looked the waiter in the face, he was serious, "How? Why? I just want to sit here and wait for a call," I said, "I want my seat by the window".

"Well today, that probably won't happen. Unless his girlfriend turns up pretty soon. She's missing, and he's worried. He doesn't look like it, but he is one angry gangster," Said the waiter," You want more coffee?".

I went a little cold in the heart.

"How do you know he's a gangster?"

"Everybody recognises that guy as a gangster. He has a reputation, you know, gangsters like that kind of publicity," Said the waiter. He finished wiping the table, then went to get my second cup of coffee.

A mobile phone vibrated in my left pocket. I pulled it out, and a voice spoke, "Hi, everything looks good. Progress on that new campaign," The voice said.

I thought for a moment. This was taking longer than I'd planned, "Well, he'll get it, when he gives me what I want — he knows how it all works. Motivate him a little," I pushed the 'off' button and placed the phone back into my jacket pocket. And waited.

The coffee tasted good, the rain stopped and started. And the woman at the back of the cafe was too quiet.

The thing about gangsters is — I think a lot about these things while I'm waiting — is that gangsters have big egos. That ego wants respect, so they force people to respect them. The problem is that respect and fear are easily mixed up. If you don't keep your self-respect, then you can't see the difference between the two. And, you end up demanding fear instead of respect.

Fear breeds mistrust, and people will plot and scheme behind your back. So, gangsters like the one sitting in front of me, end up being sitting ducks for anybody who wants what they've got.

I'm glad I don't live like him. Over blown, loud, obnoxious, public. All those things are his fears. It works for a while, then it all comes undone. Anybody who lives with so much fear can't help but look for someone to trust.

That's why he's sitting right there in my seat, all edgy and fearful — even though he hides it well. He's lost the one person he trusts, his girlfriend. A gangster like him falls for a woman, he thinks he can trust her. Then he finds he can't. His heart is warmed, but he doesn't show it. A gangster who lets another person put warmth into his heart, is a dead gangster.

Well, like I said, I think a lot about people and their ways.

My phone rang, so I picked it up.

"What's happening now, any more progress?" I asked.

"Yeah, sure. He's getting a call in a minute or two, his guys signed everything for us. We own it all now." Said the voice.

"Okay, sounds good to me. Bring her round, let him see her," I ordered.

The gangster in 'my seat' hunched his shoulders. He looked tired and sick, done. His time was short now, but he couldn't know that, his ego was too big to see.

His phone buzzed, he gently lifted it and listened. I knew what was being said. I'd told *the voice* to be courteous, so he was. Just show respect, and then get some back.

I watched as the gangster's eyes widened, he breathed out, said something, and put the phone down.

A car pulled up at the curbside, it double parked so as not to get jammed in.

The rear door opened and a woman got out. I could see the attraction. Stylish. One of my associates then guided her to the left of the car. The driver leaned out and waved at the gangster sitting in my seat, so he stood up and walked outside. He immediately hugged and kissed the woman, my associate then pulled her back into the car. The door closed.

You could see her face at the window. She feigned shock, a little drama on her side. People lie. She knew about everything.

The car drove away, then my associate walked away just as fast. The contractor looked like he was anybody, just passing by, but he went up to the gangster and fired two shots into him. He fell like a sack of apples onto the wet concrete street.

Everybody but the waiter and I left the scene. The cops came, people stopped and gawked.

It took an hour to get the mess cleaned up out there on the street. A couple of cops stood around in rain, they chatted and made jokes.

The waiter served me coffee, and wiped his brow as he told me how terrible it was, that thing that happened out there on the street.

The waiter brought me my third coffee, I dragged my chair out and sat at the window table.

Don't miss out!

Visit the website below and you can sign up to receive emails whenever Sean Patrick Durham publishes a new book. There's no charge and no obligation.

https://books2read.com/r/B-A-VOIK-ZRSRB

BOOKS2READ

Connecting independent readers to independent writers.